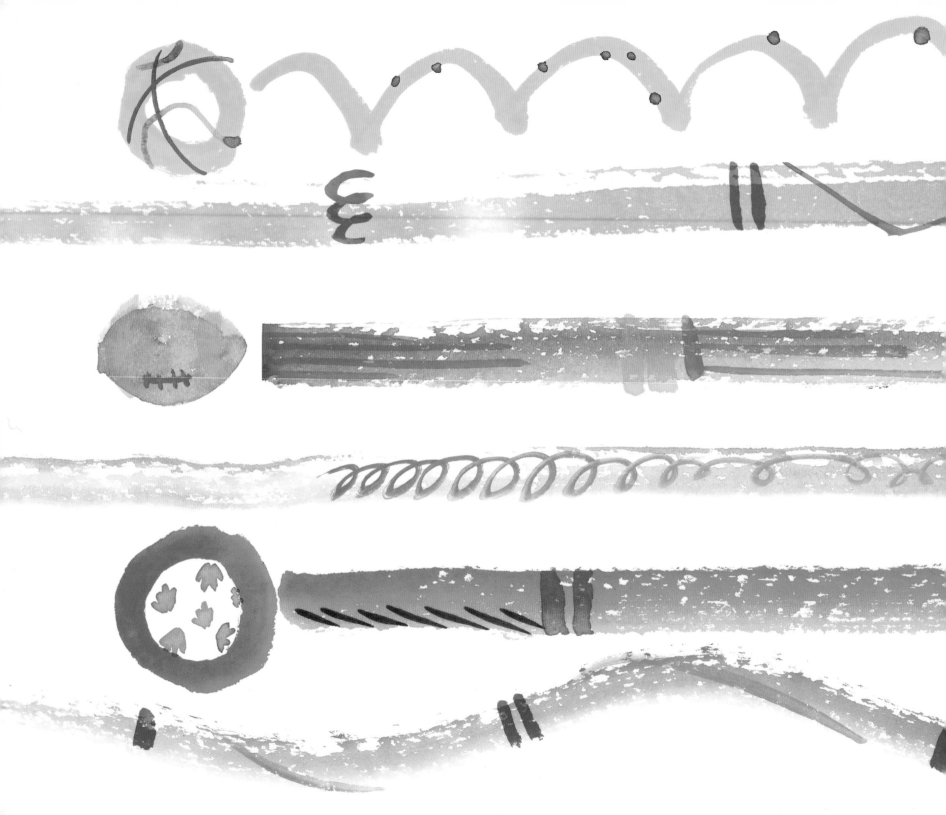

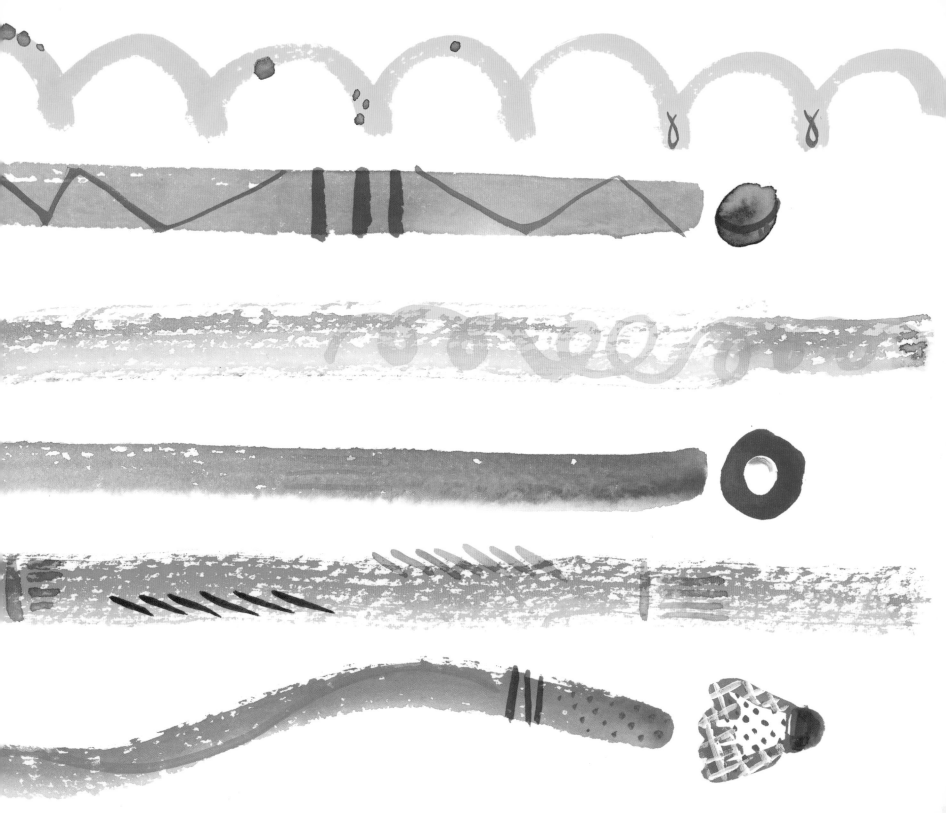

good sports

rhymes about
running, jumping, throwing,
and more

by jack prelutsky

illustrations by chris raschka

Dragonfly Books ——✤— New York

I'm standing at home,
And the count's three and two.
A fastball is coming,
And here's what I'll do—
I'll swing at that ball,
And I'll smack it so hard,
I'll send that ball sailing
Clean out of the yard.

Here comes the pitch
Heading straight for the plate . . .
I've got to swing now,
I can't wait, I can't wait.
I whiff on that fastball,
The ump yells, "Strike three!"
I'll get him *next* inning,
You just wait and see.

The ball comes to me,
And I kick the ball back.
We're looking to score,
So we're on the attack.
We slip past defenders
With sure-footed play,
Till only the goalkeeper
Stands in our way.

I pass to a teammate
Who shoots . . . it looks wide.
The goalkeeper lunges,
But luck's on *our* side.
The ball hits a goalpost,
Then goes in the net—
We're down only ten,
And may win this game yet.

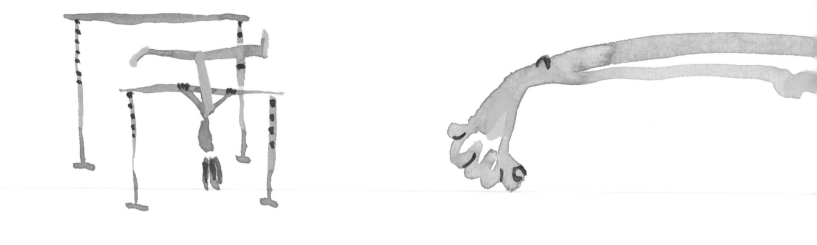

I'm a gymnast,
I can vault,
Swing and spring
And somersault,
Even balance
On the beam—
Someday soon
I'll make the team.

I'm at the foul line, and I bet
The ball will go right through the net.
I'm certain I will sink this shot,
For I've been practicing a lot.

I concentrate, then let it go . . .
I know it's good—I know, I know.
It makes an arc, I make a wish,
Then hear the soft, sweet sound of SWISH!

I'm chasing after porpoises,
I'm racing after seals.
I try to catch a walrus
And some underwater eels.

I'm an orca, I'm a marlin,
I'm a shark beneath the sea . . .
But when I surface in the pool,
I'm back to being me.

Though I like to swim,
I don't swim very well.
I swim like a fish
That's been sick for a spell.
I flop in the pool,
And I flounder around.
My friends laugh and say
I should stay on the ground.

It takes me forever
To cross the pool once.
When it comes to swimming,
I'm clearly a dunce.
But still I enjoy it
And happily think
I don't do so badly . . .
At least I don't sink!

I've got the ball, and now I need
To race downfield with all my speed,
To dodge and duck and slip and twist,
To fool the defense, make them miss.

I'm almost in the end zone now,
And still untouched . . . I don't know how.
I score a touchdown, and we've won.
I love football. Football's fun.

I just caught a pass
And I'm well on my way.
I think I will score
Seven touchdowns today.

Oh no! I've been tackled—
I fumble the ball.
I don't like this game,
Not a bit, not at all.

My friend and I play Frisbee
In the summer in the park.
I flip the Frisbee to her,
It describes a graceful arc.

She runs and tries to catch it,
And I watch her miss and fall—
We both like playing Frisbee,
Though we aren't good at all.

I rise in the air
Like a silver balloon.
I'm light as a zephyr
En route to the moon.

I whirl and I twirl,
Every move is precise—
I'm out of this world
When I'm skating on ice.

We're in the blocks
And hear the gun.
We get out fast
And run run run.

Seconds later
We're all done
And out of breath . . .
Who won? Who won?

I'm skating down the sidewalk,
I'm a meteor on wheels.
I'm faster than an asteroid,
At least, that's how it feels.

I zoom past slower skaters
Till I'm clearly in the lead—
I'm skating down the sidewalk,
The epitome of speed.

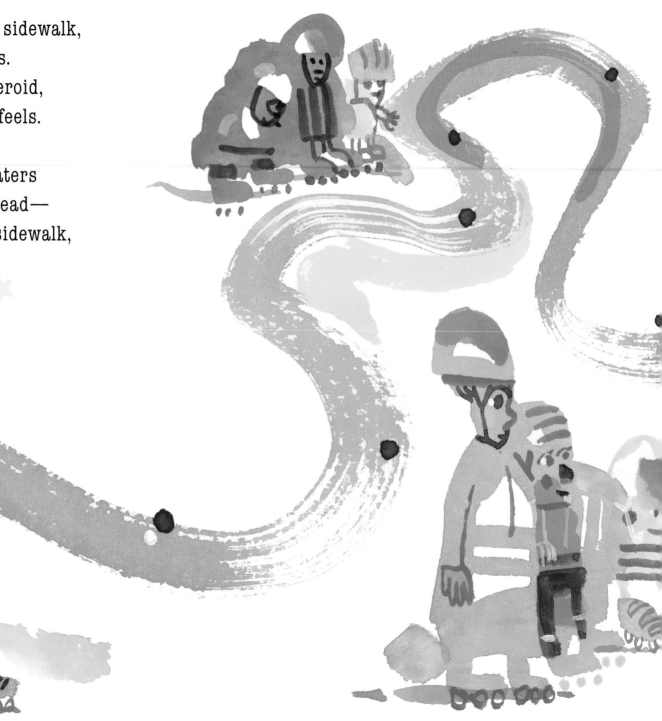

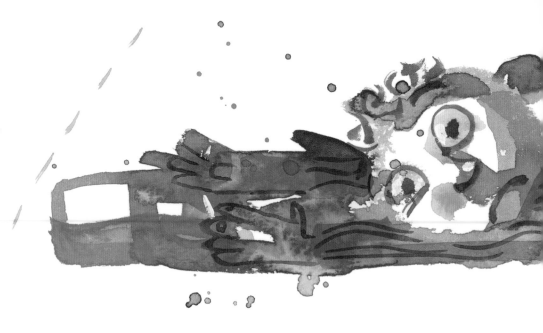

I had to slide into the plate,
It was my only chance.
Though if I hadn't slid, then I
Would not have lost my pants.

The batter hits the ball my way,
I watch it sail aloft.
I miss the catch, it hits my head—
A softball *isn't* soft!

I didn't beat the throw to first,
And now my face is red.
Next time when I'm on second base,
I'll run to third instead.

I'm going to dunk this basketball,
I'll soar above the rim.
I'll fly so high that everyone
Will cry out, "Look at him!"

My dunk will be spectacular—
The greatest of them all.
When I grow three feet taller,
I will dunk this basketball.

I'm running in a distance race,
The competition's tough.
I've never run this hard before,
And hope I've got enough.
I'm in the middle of the pack,
It's time to make my move . . .
I drift into the outside lane
And get into my groove.

The bell just sounded, and that means
We're on the final lap.
I put a burst of speed on,
And I open up a gap.
My legs are sore, I pant and pant,
I can't keep up this pace—
But now I cross the finish line,
And I have won this race.

I'm waiting here in center field,
And getting really bored.
For no one hits a thing to me—
I feel a bit ignored.

Then suddenly a high fly ball
Comes heading straight my way.
I barely catch it in my glove . . .
Once more I've saved the day.

I race toward the hoop
And I catch a good pass.
I throw the ball up
And it banks off the glass.

It rattles around
With a bit too much fuss,
Then finally falls in—
Score a couple for us.

The ball game is over,
And here is the score—
They got ninety-seven,
We got ninety-four.

Baseball is fun,
But it gives me the blues
To score ninety-four
And still manage to lose.

I chop chop chop without a stop,
I move with great agility.
I break a brick with one quick kick—
Karate . . . that's the sport for me!

To Susie Chalker,
a good sport
—J.P.

For Lefty
—C.R.

Text copyright © 2007 by Jack Prelutsky
Illustrations copyright © 2007 by Chris Raschka

Dragonfly Books with the colophon is a registered trademark of Random House, Inc.

Visit us on the Web! www.randomhouse.com/kids

Educators and librarians, for a variety of teaching tools, visit us at www.randomhouse.com/teachers

The Library of Congress has cataloged the hardcover edition of this work as follows:
Good sports / by Jack Prelutsky ; illustrated by Chris Raschka.
p. cm.
ISBN 978-0-375-83700-5 (trade) — ISBN 978-0-375-93700-2 (lib. bdg.)
[1. Sports—Juvenile poetry. 2. Children's poetry, American.] I. Raschka, Christopher. II. Title.
PS3566.R36 G66 2007
811'.54—dc22
2006005092

ISBN 978-0-375-86558-9 (pbk.)

MANUFACTURED IN CHINA

10 9 8 7 6 5 4 3 2 1

First Dragonfly Books Edition